THE PRESIDENT OF THE UNITED STATES

by Martha E. H. Rustad

PEBBLE
a capstone imprint

Pebble Explore is published by Pebble, an imprint of Capstone.
1710 Roe Crest Drive
North Mankato, Minnesota 56003
www.capstonepub.com

Library of Congress Cataloging-in-Publication Data is available on the Library of Congress website.
ISBN 978-1-9771-1395-5 (hardcover)
ISBN 978-1-9771-1820-2 (paperback)
ISBN 978-1-9771-1404-4 (ebook pdf)

Summary: Describes the president's duties, the White House, how the President is elected, and more.

Photo Credits
Library of Congress Prints and Photographs Division, 24, 25, 27; NARA, 26; Newscom: Everett Collection, 7, 19, Pete Souza - White House via CNP, 16, Reuters/Mike Blake, 13. UPI Photo Service/Lee K. Marriner, 9, ZUMA Press/Apec Pool, 5, ZUMA Press/Eric Draper, 17, ZUMA Press/Evan Sayles, 11, ZUMA Press/Ricky Bassman, 10, ZUMA Press/White House, 21; Pete Souza, The Obama-Biden Transition Project, 28; Shutterstock: Everett - Art, 22, Everett Historical, 23, Realest Nature, Cover; US Airforce, 15

Design Elements
Shutterstock: ExpressVectors, In-Finity

Editorial Credits
Anna Butzer, editor; Cynthia Della-Rovere, designer;
Jo Miller, media researcher; Laura Manthe, production specialist

All internet sites appearing in back matter were available and accurate when this book was sent to press.

Printed and bound in China.
2489

Table of Contents

Words in **bold** are in the glossary.

What Is a President?

Imagine a job where you are in charge. You make important decisions. Leaders around the world want to meet with you. You are in charge of the **military**. You can help make rules called laws. Who are you? The President of the United States!

The president often meets with leaders of other countries.

The president leads the U.S. government. A government makes rules for the country to follow. The U.S. government is a **democracy**. People get to choose their leaders. Leaders work together to make the country better.

Presidents promise to do the best job that they can.

Who Can Be President?

Do you want to lead the United States? There a few rules about who can get the job. Presidents must have been born in this country, or their parents must have been born here. They must be at least 35 years old. They must have lived in the United States for at least 14 years.

George W.
BUSH
FOR PRESIDENT

How Are Presidents Chosen?

Many people want to become president. They share their ideas with others. They listen to different ideas. They talk about ways to fix problems. They talk about ways to make the country better.

A candidate listens to people's thoughts and ideas.

People then decide who will be the final **candidates** running for office. These candidates go across the country to share their ideas and plans. They let people know why they want to lead the country.

People **vote** for the next president on **Election** Day. It is the second Tuesday in November. They decide who will lead the country.

The winner becomes president and holds the job for four years. After four years, there is another election. Presidents can be elected two times and be in office up to eight years.

People vote for the candidate that they think will do the best job.

Where Do Presidents Work?

The U.S. government meets in the capital city of Washington, D.C. The president lives and works there in the White House. The president's office is the shape of an oval. It is called the Oval Office.

The president has a team of people who work in the White House. They write speeches for the president. They answer phone calls and share information with the president.

Air Force One

The president travels all over the world. An airplane called Air Force One flies the president everywhere. The president can work on the plane. The plane even has a bed for overnight trips.

There are 132 rooms, 35 bathrooms, and six floors in the White House. The president's family lives on two of the floors. Many presidents have had pets in the White House too.

The president takes time to relax after work. There is a theater where the president and their family can watch movies. There is also a bowling alley, a swimming pool, and basketball courts!

What Do Presidents Do?

The president works to make the country better. A president's job is not easy. The president works long, busy days. There are phone calls to make and notes to read.

The president must meet with their team and members of **Congress**. A president also gives speeches and goes to important events.

Lawmakers send bills to the president. A bill is a plan for a new law. When the president signs a bill, it becomes a law. The president can **veto** any law. Then lawmakers have to make a new plan.

The president must make important decisions. People in a group called the **cabinet** help with this job. They talk with the president. They help make decisions.

The president also leads the U.S. military. Military groups help keep the country safe. The president works with military leaders. They give the president advice.

The president is in charge of the military.

The president works with different parts of the government to pass laws. They talk about how to work together. They help each other solve our country's problems.

Famous Presidents

FIRST PRESIDENT

George Washington was the first president of the United States. He served for eight years. He is the only president that didn't live in the White House. It was built after he left office.

George Washington

Thomas Jefferson

THOMAS JEFFERSON

Thomas Jefferson was president for eight years. As president, he helped buy land that would double the size of the country.

ABRAHAM LINCOLN

Abraham Lincoln was president from 1861 to 1865. He kept the United States together during a time of war.

Abraham Lincoln

YOUNGEST PRESIDENT, OLDEST PRESIDENT

Theodore Roosevelt was the youngest president. He was 42 years old when he became president. The oldest president was Ronald Regan. He was 77 years old when his **term** ended.

Franklin D. Roosevelt

LONGEST TERM

President Franklin D. Roosevelt was elected to four terms. The rules changed after he was in office. Now a president can serve only one or two terms.

SHORTEST TERM

President William Henry Harrison served the shortest term. He died after being in office for only 31 days.

William Henry Harrison

FIRST AFRICAN AMERICAN PRESIDENT

Barack Obama was the 44th president and the first African American president. He was president for eight years.

Barack Obama

Fast Facts

Role: The President

Job: The president works for the country's people in Washington, D.C.

How Presidents Are Chosen: People vote for president every four years. A president's term lasts four years. Presidents can serve up to two terms.

Pay: The first presidents earned $25,000 per year. Today presidents earn $400,000 per year.

Glossary

bill (BIL)—a written idea for a new law

cabinet (KA-buh-nit)—a group of people that help the president make sure that people follow rules and laws

candidate (KAN-duh-dayt)—a person who wants a job in government

Congress (KAHNG-gruhs)—the group of people who make the laws for the United States

democracy (di-MAH-kruh-see)—a kind of government; citizens choose people to work for them

election (i-LEK-shuhn)—the act of choosing people to work in government

military (MIL-uh-ter-ee)—the armed forces of a state or country

term (TERM)—a set amount of time for a job

veto (VEE-toh)—to choose not to sign a bill into law

vote (VOHT)—to make a choice in a group decision based on your views

Read More

Alexander, Vincent. *Executive Branch.* Minneapolis: Jump!, 2019.

Krasner, Barbara. *Exploring the Executive Branch.* Minneapolis: Lerner, 2020.

Pagel-Hogan, Elizabeth. *So You Want to be President of the United States.* North Mankato, MN: Capstone Press, 2019.

Internet Sites

How the President Is Elected
http://www.socialstudiesforkids.com/articles/government/howthepresidentiselected.htm

The White House: Presidents
https://www.whitehouse.gov/about-the-white-house/presidents/

USA.gov: Branches of the U.S. Government
https://www.usa.gov/branches-of-government

Index